INKY'S AMAZING ESCAPE

How a Very Smart Octopus Found His Way Home

Illustrated by Amy Schimler-Safford

Sy Montgomery

WITHDRAWN

WITHDRAWN

A Paula Wiseman Book
Simon & Schuster Books for Young Readers
New York London Toronto Sydney New Delhi

The baby octopus hatched out of an egg
the size of a grain of rice. His mother used her
jet to blow him from her den out to the sea,
along with his tiny octopus brothers and sisters.

Each octopus set out on a journey alone.
They're born ready to explore.

For weeks the octopus rode the currents of the Pacific Ocean.
He ate tiny scraps of food that floated by.
He grew fast.

Soon he needed bigger meals: clams, fish—and octopuses'
favorite—crabs. To find them, the little octopus had to explore.

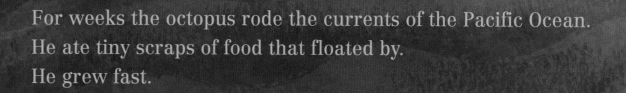

Curious, he wondered: Might there be a tasty morsel
here? What about over there? He poked his slippery,
bendy arms into every nook and cranny. Soon he
found a yummy clam. He used his strong suckers to
pull the clam apart, and ate the clam for dinner.

Now the octopus was sleepy.
How would he find a safe place to nap?

He searched among the coral. He found a
crack that lead to a little cave. In went
one, arm, two arms, four arms—eight.
Good night!

In the morning the octopus again went exploring. What would he find today? He could both feel and taste with his suckers.

But he didn't see the long green fish swimming like a banner rippling in the wind. It was a moray eel. He chomped down on two of the octopus's arms!
The young octopus used his jet to shoot away, head first, arms trailing behind.

But the eel had bitten off the tips of two arms.
The octopus was hungry and hurt, but he went on.

The octopus spotted a wooden box lying on the
seafloor. In went his slippery, bendy arms.
In went his squishy head. He ate the lobster.
Then he took a nap.

Woken from sleep, the octopus felt himself rising up and out of the water. What the octopus thought was a safe den was a fisherman's lobster trap.

"You aren't a lobster!" the fisherman exclaimed. "Who do we have here?"
The octopus, who had never seen a human before, wondered the same thing.
"You're hurt!" the lobsterman observed.

He decided to take the little octopus to the aquarium.

The aquarium keeper saw the octopus's hurt arms. "You'll be safe with us!" she told the octopus, and poured him into a tank. She named him Inky, because when they're scared, octopuses can squirt ink.

But the little octopus wasn't scared. He was ready to explore. He felt and tasted the glass and all the corners with his slippery, bendy arms and his strong suckers. He crawled to the top of the tank and looked up at the keeper. She handed him his favorite snack: a yummy crab. Now they were friends.

Inky liked it when the keeper petted him. Sometimes he was so happy he would change color. Octopuses change color to fool prey and escape enemies, but they show their feelings this way, too.

When the keeper opened the lid to his tank, Inky turned red with excitement. When he relaxed, he turned white.

Sometimes he made
spots on his arms.

Sometimes he sprouted
stripes and splotches.

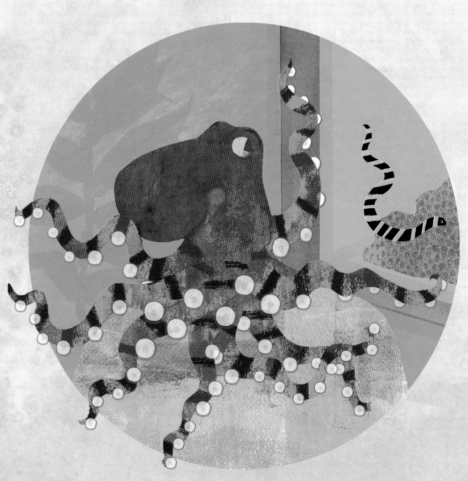

Inky felt better. He had fun in his tank. The keeper gave him dried corals, pots, and jars to explore. Inky poked his slippery, bendy arms into all of them. Sometimes he'd squeeze his squishy head inside.

Sometimes the keeper gave Inky toys. Inky liked to take apart LEGO blocks, and put them back together.

He liked playing with Mr. Potato Head. One time, with his suckers, he pulled off Mr. Potato Head's eyes, and handed them to the starfish in his tank.

Inky grew very fast. When he arrived at the aquarium he was the size of a baseball. Now he was the size of a soccer ball. His arms had healed!

Inky was always exploring. One night the keeper forgot to close the lid to Inky's tank tightly enough.

He poked a slippery, bendy arm through the gap. What would he find?

First one arm, then another, and another—then all eight arms climbed out of the tank. Finally his squishy head was out, too.

Inky slid along the floor, exploring with his arms. Soon he came to a hole—a drain for the water always slopping out of aquarium tanks and hoses. Where would the hole lead? There was only one way to find out.

He poked his slippery, bendy arms into the drain. One arm, two arms, four arms—eight! He pulled and pushed, he pushed and pulled—and finally his squishy head popped inside the drain too.

Inky traveled a long way. Down, down, and down, Inky inched his way through the long pipe. At last, he could feel and taste a change.

Out popped one arm, two arms, four arms—eight—and finally Inky's squishy head was free again! The drainpipe ran right back into the Pacific Ocean.

And that's where Inky is today—still ready to explore.

Endnote

Inky was a real octopus. The lobsterman who caught him off New Zealand's shallow reefs donated him to the National Aquarium in Wellington. Inky's nighttime escape down the drain and back to the sea in 2016 was reported in newspapers around the world.

Octopuses are fabulous escape artists. They have only one hard part in the body—the beak—and can squeeze through any opening big enough to fit it. (That's how Inky, big as a soccer ball, could squeeze through a drainpipe that was only six inches wide.) Their muscles are less like our biceps and more like our tongues. (You can stick your tongue partway into the neck of a bottle—but couldn't do it with your bicep, even if you could detach it from your arm bone!) Slime covering the skin makes the octopus slippery and also keeps its skin moist during short overland excursions. Suckers on the arms help propel the animal across any surface, wet or dry.

There are many stories about octopuses that have left their tanks to go exploring.

One story goes like this: At Brighton, England's public aquarium, staffers noticed fish disappearing from the tank next to the one housing their octopus. What happened? Where did the fish go? It remained a mystery—until one morning, they found the octopus in the lumpfish tank. Apparently the octopus had been escaping each night to feed on his neighbors, and returning to his own tank before people could find out!

Because they lack bones, octopuses can squeeze through unbelievably small openings. A collector searching for specimens for the American Museum of Natural History once caught a foot-long octopus in Puerto Rico. He secured the octopus in a cigar box. He hammered the lid down with tacks. He wound a cord around the box tightly. But when he went to open the box again, it was empty. He found the octopus later, in the water in the bottom of the boat, hiding near an oar.

Certainly that octopus didn't want to live in a cigar box, with no water! But what about other octopuses in captivity? Are they unhappy in public aquariums? Did Inky escape to regain his freedom? Was he lonely?

Inky was probably very happy in his tank at the aquarium. He had plenty to do. He wasn't bored. He wasn't lonely. (Most species of octopus are solitary anyway. Even when it comes time for mating, there's always a danger one will eat the other!)

Then why might Inky, and these other octopuses, escape?

The answer is simple: Because they're curious. Octopuses love to explore.

After all, Christopher Columbus didn't set sail across the ocean because he didn't like Spain. Astronauts don't go to outer space because they don't like Earth. And some species of octopus are known to sometimes purposely leave the shallows of the ocean and crawl out on land for a little while. That's not because they don't like the water.

Even though you don't look much like an octopus, you are probably alike in some ways. And this is one of them: Both of you are smart, curious creatures, eager to discover what else is out there.

8 Fun Octopus Facts

1. There are more than 250 different kinds of octopus. One kind, the Star Sucker Pygmy Octopus, is so small that a grown-up one would fit on your fingertip. The largest, the Giant Pacific Octopus, can grow to 300 pounds. Inky was a Common New Zealand Octopus.

2. An octopus can change color. He or she can make spots or stripes or splotches appear on the skin. The octopus can turn red or white or brown. Some octopuses can also turn bright blue, or green, or yellow, or even purple—and change color again in less than a second. Some can even glow in the dark.

3. An octopus can also change shape. Octopuses have no bones, so they can squeeze their squishy, baggy bodies into tiny spaces. A 100-pound octopus can squeeze through an opening the size of an orange! They can also make big bumps and even "horns" on the surface of their skin—all in an instant.

4. Yum: An octopus can taste with his skin. Even his eyelids! But the sense of taste is most developed in the suckers on the inside of the arms.

5. Those suckers are super strong. A single sucker the size of a silver dollar can lift twenty pounds. An octopus can have hundreds of suckers on each of his or her eight arms. And they are so flexible that an octopus can use suckers like we use our fingers—even to untie knotted thread.

6. An octopus's body is very different from a person's. Octopuses have three hearts, blue blood, and a brain that wraps around his throat. The part of the octopus that looks like a head isn't really a head. It's more like our middle, where the octopus's stomach is. And the mouth is in the armpits!

7. To protect itself, an octopus can shoot ink. The ink blob hangs in the water and looks sort of like an octopus. The predator stares at the octo-blob while the actual octopus changes color and jets away.

8. If a predator bites off part of an octopus's arm—or even the entire arm—the octopus can regrow it, like new.

Suggestions for Further Reading

An Octopus Is Amazing by Patricia Lauber. HarperCollins. 1996.

The Octopus Scientists: Exploring the Mind of a Mollusk by Sy Montgomery and photos by Keith Ellenbogen. Harcourt Houghton Mifflin, 2015.

Octopus: The Ocean's Intelligent Invertebrate by Roland C. Anderson and Jennifer A. Mather. Timber Press, 2010.

Inky's Escape was International News. Here are some of the stories you may find interesting:
https://www.nytimes.com/2016/04/14/world/asia/inky-octopus-new-zealand-aquarium.html
http://www.npr.org/2016/04/16/474412283/inky-the-octopuss-great-escape
https://www.theguardian.com/environment/video/2016/apr/13/inky-octopus-escapes-tank-video
http://news.nationalgeographic.com/2016/04/160414-inky-octopus-escapes-intelligence/

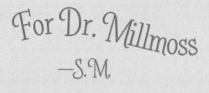

For Dr. Millmoss
—S. M.

For the other Sy, Flo, and our ocean home
—A. S.

SIMON & SCHUSTER BOOKS FOR YOUNG READERS

An imprint of Simon & Schuster Children's Publishing Division

1230 Avenue of the Americas, New York, New York 10020

Text copyright © 2018 by Sy Montgomery • Illustrations copyright © 2018 by Amy Schimler-Safford

SIMON & SCHUSTER BOOKS FOR YOUNG READERS is a trademark of Simon & Schuster, Inc.

For information about special discounts for bulk purchases, please contact Simon & Schuster Special

Sales at 1-866-506-1949 or business@simonandschuster.com.

The Simon & Schuster Speakers Bureau can bring authors to your live event. For more information or to book an event, contact the

Simon & Schuster Speakers Bureau at 1-866-248-3049 or visit our website at www.simonspeakers.com.

Book design by Chloë Foglia • The text for this book was set in Centennial.

The illustrations for this book were created using mixed media: watercolor, gouache, acrylics,

and oil pastel on special papers and collaged along with found paper, then finished digitally.

Manufactured in China • 0618 SCP • First Edition

2 4 6 8 10 9 7 5 3 1

Library of Congress Cataloging-in-Publication Data

Names: Montgomery, Sy, author. | Schimler-Safford, Amy, illustrator.

Title: Inky's amazing escape : how a very smart octopus found his way home / Sy Montgomery ; illustrated by Amy Schimler-Safford.

Description: First edition. | New York : Simon & Schuster Books for Young Readers, [2018] |

Audience: Age 4–8. | Audience: K to Grade 3. | A Paula Wiseman Book.

Identifiers: LCCN 2017061227| ISBN 9781534401914 (hardcover) | ISBN 9781534401921 (eBook)

Subjects: LCSH: Octopuses—New Zealand—Anecdotes—Juvenile literature. | Aquarium animals—Juvenile literature.

Classification: LCC QL430.3.O2 M65 2018 | DDC 594/.560993—dc23 • LC record available at https://lccn.loc.gov/2017061227